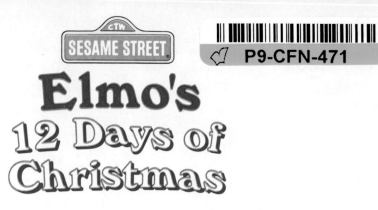

SESAME STREET

Elmo's 12 Days of Christmas

By Sarah Albee
Illustrated by Maggie Swanson

Featuring Jim Henson's Sesame Street Muppets

A SESAME STREET/GOLDEN BOOK

Published by Western Publishing Company, Inc.,
in conjunction with Children's Television Workshop

© 1996 Children's Television Workshop. Jim Henson's Sesame Street Muppet Characters © 1996 Jim Henson Productions, Inc. All rights reserved. Printed in the U.S.A. No part of this book may be reproduced or copied in any form without written permission from the copyright owner. Sesame Street and the Sesame Street Sign are trademarks and service marks of Children's Television Workshop. All other trademarks are the property of Western Publishing Company, Inc. Library of Congress Catalog Card Number: 96-75580   ISBN: 0-307-98787-6   A MCMXCVI   First Edition 1996

A portion of the money you pay for this book goes to
Children's Television Workshop. It is put right back into
SESAME STREET and other CTW educational projects.
Thanks for helping!

On the first day of Christmas
My true love gave to me one red monster up in a tree!

On the second day of Christmas
My true love gave to me two yummy cookies
And a red monster up in a tree.

On the third day of Christmas
My true love gave to me three French friends,
Two yummy cookies,
And a red monster up in a tree.

On the fourth day of Christmas
My true love gave to me four calling monsters,

Three French friends, two yummy cookies,
And a red monster up in a tree.

On the fifth day of Christmas
My true love gave to me five golden things,

Four calling monsters, three French friends,
   two yummy cookies,
And a red monster up in a tree.

On the sixth day of Christmas
My true love gave to me six monsters playing,

Five golden things, four calling monsters,
 three French friends, two yummy cookies,
And a red monster up in a tree.

On the seventh day of Christmas
My true love gave to me seven monsters swimming,

Six monsters playing, five golden things,
   four calling monsters, three French friends,
   two yummy cookies,
And a red monster up in a tree.

On the eighth day of Christmas
My true love gave to me eight monsters milking,

Seven monsters swimming, six monsters playing,
five golden things, four calling monsters,
three French friends, two yummy cookies,
And a red monster up in a tree.

On the ninth day of Christmas
My true love gave to me nine monsters dancing,

Eight monsters milking, seven monsters
    swimming, six monsters playing,
    five golden things, four calling monsters,
    three French friends, two yummy cookies,
And a red monster up in a tree.

On the tenth day of Christmas
My true love gave to me ten monsters leaping,

Nine monsters dancing, eight monsters milking,
   seven monsters swimming, six monsters
   playing, five golden things, four calling monsters,
   three French friends, two yummy cookies,
And a red monster up in a tree.

On the eleventh day of Christmas
My true love gave to me eleven monsters piping,

Ten monsters leaping, nine monsters dancing,
   eight monsters milking, seven monsters
   swimming, six monsters playing, five golden
   things, four calling monsters, three French friends,
   two yummy cookies,
And a red monster up in a tree.

On the twelfth day of Christmas
My true love gave to me twelve monsters
drumming,

Eleven monsters piping, ten monsters leaping,
nine monsters dancing, eight monsters milking,
seven monsters swimming, six monsters playing,
five golden things, four calling monsters, three
French friends, two yummy cookies,
And a red monster up in a tree.

Next time maybe we should just sing "Deck the Halls"!